To

....

HAPPY
EASTER

Love

....

THE EASTER BUNNY
is coming to
MICHIGAN

Written by Eric James   Illustrated by Mari Lobo

The sweet Easter Bunny
is skipping along,
heading through Michigan
singing this song:

GREAT LAKES TOYS

OPEN

Wolverine
State
Easter
Parade
TODAY!

Cakes

U.P. BOOKS

TINY THE **Michigan** EASTER BUNNY

THE Littlest Bunny IN Michigan

"The eggs are delivered.
My Easter job's done.
And now it is time
that I joined in the fun!"

She jumps down a tunnel
that runs underground,
and pops up again
in each city and town.

Petoskey, Holland,
Saginaw, too.
I bet there's a tunnel
that's very near you!

In Grand Rapids young children
have smiles on their faces,
and eggs decorated
like people and places!

But one little boy
drops the egg from his hands.
A loud **CRACKING** sound
can be heard as it lands.

"Oh dear!" says the bunny,
and dabs at a tear.
"You need cheering up
so thank goodness I'm here!"

She wiggles her ears,
she hops on the spot,
she waggles her tail,
and he giggles a lot!

In Lansing, there is
an Easter parade.
Most children are clapping
but one looks afraid.

That clapping is noisy.
These legs are so TALL!
It's crowded and loud,
and she's ever so small!

"Gee whiz, what a din!
I know just what to do.
Come here little one
and I'll hold hands with you!"

She wiggles her ears,
and spins her around.
The little girl laughs
as her feet leave the ground!

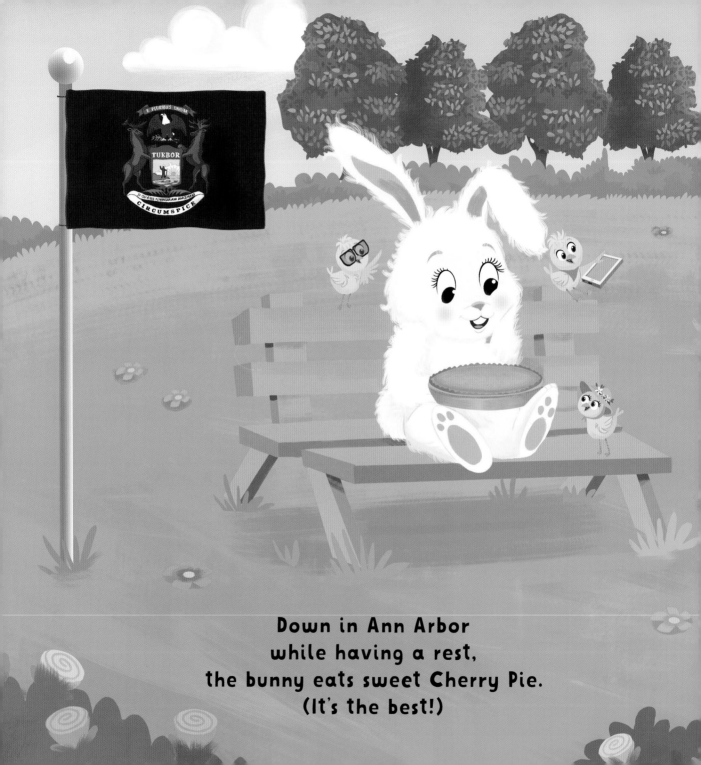

Down in Ann Arbor
while having a rest,
the bunny eats sweet Cherry Pie.
(It's the best!)

Across in the park
there's an egg-rolling race.
A small boy falls down
and he's now lost his place!

The bunny trips up
as she's going to help.
She falls down the hill
with an **OUCH** and a **YELP!**

YELP!

OUCH!

She's just a big blur
as she tumbles on past.
The boy runs to help her.
He's going so FAST!

FINISH

She wiggles her ears,
he can't (but he tries!).
They hop up and down
for they've just won first prize!

In Detroit, a girl's lost
her favorite stuffed bear.
Where could she have left him?
She's looked everywhere!

Apple
Blossoms
just in!

"When I'm feeling sad
do you know what I do?
I hop up and down!
Do you want to try too?"

She wiggles her ears, the girl thinks it's funny,
and laughs even more when she hops like a bunny!

They both jump around like they haven't a care.
And look what the chicks have just found, over there!

In Traverse City, the bunny
helps children with SHARING.

In Sault Ste. Marie, she helps
a child be DARING.

MACKINAC ISLAND

In Marquette she SINGS,
in Kalamazoo she WIGGLES.

Wherever she goes
she brings LAUGHTER and GIGGLES!

This day's been so busy
but also such fun.
The bunny daydreams
in the warm setting sun.

The twilight is coming,
the three chicks are lazing,
and tweeting about
how this day's been #AMAZING!

The bunny jumps up,
snapping out of her daze,
"There's only three-hundred-
and-sixty-four days!"

More chocolate needs making!
New eggs will need wrapping!
It's all so exciting,
the three chicks start flapping!

"Michigan's great
and we love being here.
We'll make lots more eggs
and we'll be back
next year!"

She wrinkles her nose,
she wiggles her ears,
she blows you a kiss,
and she just...disappears!

Written by Eric James
Illustrated by Mari Lobo
Additional artwork by Gisela Bohórquez
Designed by Nicky Scott

Published by Sourcebooks Wonderland,
an imprint of Sourcebooks Kids
P.O. Box 4410, Naperville, Illinois 60567-4410
(630) 961-3900
sourcebookskids.com

Date of Production: August 2019
Run Number: 5015369
Printed and bound in China (1010)
10 9 8 7 6 5 4 3 2 1